MO

Adventures in the Liaden Universe® Number 20

A Liaden Universe® novelette

Sharon Lee and Steve Miller

Pinbeam Books

http://www.pinbeambooks.com

COPYRIGHT PAGE

Moon's Honor

Moon's Honor first published at Splinter Universe (www.splinteruniverse.com), February 1, 2012

On Casting your Fate to the Moon, is original to this publication

ISBN: 978-1-935224-98-3

Published August 2013 by Pinbeam Books

Pinbeam Books

PO Box 1586

Waterville ME 04903

email info@pinbeambooks.com

Cover image from JupiterImages

Cover design by Sharon Lee

On Casting Your Fate to the Moon

The Lee-Miller writing team is often given credit for the scope, depth, and tightness of our plotting. Readers are thrilled to think that we could have *already known*, 'way back in 1984, when *Agent of Change* was written, that this-or-that seemingly random piece of business put into narrative by Val Con and Miri would be a valuable assist to Theo, in 2010, when *Ghost Ship* was written.

While we're pleased to accept any laurels tossed in our direction, what we actually deserve credit for are retentive memories and extraordinarily facile back-brains.

Because, of course we didn't—and don't—plot twenty-six years and thirteen books out. No, what we excel at isn't plotting, but *remembering* that random bit of business, and apprehending the problem to which it is an answer in the on-going tale of Clan Korval, its allies, and its enemies. Call it, if you will, *retroactive plotting.*

Of course, that's not to say that we don't plan—or plot—ahead. *Moon's Honor* is a case in point.

See, 'way back in 1984, when we were writing *Agent of Change*, and plotting out seven books in series, we were also plotting out a secondary narrative line that would include several novels. That secondary narrative would chronicle the adventures of Moonhawk and Lute, serially reincarnated characters who operate in what seems, at first, to be a fantasy world. The plan, back then, was to move that pair of characters along in time until their thread intersected with the frankly science fictional thread following Clan Korval.

Well, the publishing industry—what we'll call *reality*—didn't favor that plan—or plot. The seven-book SF thread was shot down at Book Three—we never even got a chance to propose the Lute and Moonhawk thread.

During the years in which we were out of contract, we wrote a couple short stories about the pair—see *Fellow Traveler's: Adventures in the Liaden Universe® Number 2*, available as an ebook from Amazon, BN, and Smashwords—and they of course play a strong supporting role as the allies of Rool Tiazan and his lady, in *Crystal Dragon.*

That brings us roughly to late 1996—eleven years after we laid our Grand Plan and seven years after it all fell to dust and ashes. We had written, in our copious free time, The *Tomorrow Log*, *Local Custom*, *Scout's Progress*, and *Plan B*, plus numerous short stories. And we said to ourselves something along the lines of, "Well, since we basically writing for our own amusement at this point, why not put together a proposal for the first Lute and Moonhawk novel?"

They say it's better to be busy than not, so we did that—12,000-ish words of sample chapters and an outline of how the book would proceed from there. The proposal made the rounds—and had no takers. The common editorial complaint that the story was simply too generic.

So be it. Had things gone along as they had been going along, i.e. Lee and Miller write novel; submit; every publishing house on earth rejects—we might have, many years before Kickstarter, written the book anyway (as had become our habit), to amuse ourselves and to keep our covenant with the characters.

But, things didn't go along as they had been doing. In late 1997, Meisha Merlin contacted us about reprinting the first three Liaden novels, *Agent of Change, Conflict of Honors*, and *Carpe Diem*. After negotiation, the reprinting project was parlayed into a seven-book deal, including all the books we'd written but not published to that point. Between 1998 and 2006, we published eleven novels in eight books with Meisha Merlin—which also passed on the Moonhawk and Lute thread, so as not to "dilute" the main Liaden narrative.

Which left us with. . .the first 12,000-ish words of (in our humble opinion as the fond authors) a pretty dern good novel, or! a novelette detailing one of the many "first meetings" of Lute and Moonhawk.

So, here you have it. We hope you enjoy the story.

Sharon Lee and Steve Miller
The Cat Farm and Confusion Factory
Central Maine
August 18, 2013

MOON'S HONOR

THE MOON

Caution, danger, error, disillusionment

Out of the high country it drove him, lashing him through and around places where normally he would have tarried, displayed his skill, collected a coin, an egg, a cheese.

At first he fought it, this vast and reasonless compulsion, though his master had always urged him to heed the lesser sendings he had experienced in the past.

Those had never frightened him.

This—this chilled his soul. So he fought, striving to bring his own will to the fore—and lost, as the compulsion moved him, puppet-like, down from the mountains where breath still showed frost at dawn and at sunset, into the high valleys and further, to the river plain itself, where spring was already blooming.

He must reach Dyan City by full Moon. So little to know, when one was accustomed to being one's own master. Certainly too little to keep him on his feet and traveling well into the night, with only the racing Hounds to light him. Far too little to raise him from his fireless camp at dawn's first blush, walking again as he broke his fast from the dwindling supply of journeybread.

The bread was gone by the time his feet touched the road to Dyan City, and he walked the last miles hungry, passing through the gates as they were closing for the night.

It was Beltane Eve.

The compulsion shoved him through the gate-market, past the rim of cheap inns and beer-rooms, through a ragged ring of houses, toward the city's center.

He hurried across the warehouse district, and a zone of painfully tidy houses, each with its own tiny garden spot; through the mid-point market and the streets of upscale inns; past shops and through wide cobbled streets faced by spacious houses where music and laughter spilled from walled and secret gardens. On and on his demon rode him, through odorous crowds, past perfumed pavilions, until he reached Goddess Square.

There, facing the glory of Dyan Temple, at the very foot of Maidenstairs, with the Elder Hound just rounding the Eastern Tower—there, the compulsion left him.

"Crone's teeth!" An oath, though he was not in general a man who cursed.

He swayed, so suddenly was he free, and his knees began to go. Teeth-grit, he caught himself, determined that none of the Temple should see him kneeling and mistakenly bear him inside as a suppliant.

His master had maintained that these incidents of compulsion were Goddess-sent, thus holy, and had adjured his apprentice to heed the sendings and obey them with grace.

Sadly, the 'prentice had never been so sweetly devout as the master, and endured these moments of the Goddess' favor with wariness, not to say, dislike. Endured he had, however, and learned that a foretelling of gold eventually turned golden, and a whiff of disaster held real danger. Thus, he added another weapon—chancy as it was—to his arsenal of survival. But such a compulsion as this? Never before had he experienced the like: To be herded like a cow, five days down from the mountains, neglecting both work and food—neglecting even the all-important practice!—to be dumped at the foot of Maidenstairs like a sack of wheat, without the first notion of why he should be there? His life disrupted and his stomach growling, all for the Goddess' mere whim?

He was inclined to be annoyed.

However, it was not politic to be annoyed at the foot of Maidenstairs within the heart of one of the Three Cities, and he was a man possessed of shrewdness.

Deliberately, playing for those who might be watching from tower-top or window-slit, he made obeisance, cloak swirling gracefully as he sank to one knee in the Houndlight. He held the genuflection for a long beat of three, head bowed in reverence, then came straight in one fluid movement. Carefully, he backed nine steps from the foot of Maidenstairs, his eyes on the pinnacle of the Eastern Tower.

Then, ritual flawlessly performed, he turned gently on his heel and vanished back into the city.

There was a guildhall in Dyan City, but he was not wishful of meeting his fellows thus new from the kiss of the Goddess. The few coins hoarded in the lining of his cloak were enough, he reckoned, for a meal at one of the outer inns. He trusted to his skills—rusty as they must be from so long without practice—to earn him a place near the hearth for sleeping, and a bit of sausage wrapped in fresh bread to see him along the road, tomorrow sunrise.

Mind made up and course once more his own to chose, he sauntered through the streets of Dyan City, taking leisure to look about him, now that the lash was off his back. He marked the silks, furs and fine woolens; the gilded doors and the locked gardens, gates lit by the steady glow of electric lanterns, gift of Dyan Temple's generator.

He sighed and went away from the avenues of nobles, crossed the empty evening market and passed into a gaggle of thinner streets, most lit with candle-lanterns. More folk were about here, there being no pleasure-gardens to lock themselves into, and he went freely among them.

Those who saw him at all merely marked a thin man, a bit taller than some, with a face that might have seen twenty years or forty, in the way of faces sun-browned and scoured by the winds of turning seasons. His neatly braided hair was black, showing no lighter strands; under the road dust his cloak was likewise black. He carried a bag beneath it, slung over his shoulder by a leather strap. But none passing him on the street would note that.

The inn he chose, by and by, had a remarkably lifelike carving of a snowy owl aside the door, talons gripping the wooden peg it stood upon. On the wall above someone had shakily hand painted the legend: Hunter's Moon.

He had not expected such erudition in this ring of the city and turned eagerly toward the merry red door and the wooden owl's baleful stare. He moved his hand as he did so, conjuring a bright green counter from the air. He walked it across the back of his hand, vanished it, reached out and drew it from the carven feathers on the owl's snowy cheek, grinning in unselfconscious pleasure. His fingers were not so stiff, after all.

It was then he saw the parchment.

Real parchment, such as Temple Proclamations were written on, inked in green and signed in silver, with official ribbons dangling from the pentagram that sealed it. Heart unaccountably stilled—for what did Temple Proclamations have to do with him?—he leaned forward to read it.

Let it hereby be known that all and any practitioners of the so-called "Craft Magic", which is that fraudery and sleight-of-hand designed only to trick the naive eye and beguile the foolish from the True

Wonder of the Goddess, shall fail to display these supposed arts within the sight and hearing of the Circle.

Let it also be known that any who in defiance of this order of the Temple persevere in displaying the "Craft Magic" shall be considered to have performed blasphemy and shall be schooled accordingly.

This by the order of the Inner Circle, Dyan Temple, whose will is set forth by the hand of Greenlady upon the thirty-second night of the waxing moon looking toward Beltane.

"Blasphemy." His fingers flicked, vanishing the damning counters even as he tried to breathe normally, to hide all outward signs of fear. The "schooling" that drew one away from blasphemy had to do with incarceration in some deep room within the Temple, and the constant company of those of the Circle, whose purpose it was to bring the sinner to honest abhorrence of his sin and repudiation thereof.

Some even survived the experience.

Was this why he had been driven to Dyan City? he wondered, and then shook his head. The Goddess knew each of Her children by name and every soul was as a crystal for Her scrying, so the teaching went. Armed with such knowledge, She could not for a moment have supposed that Her son Lute would gladly walk up Maidenstairs, declare himself magician and practitioner of the so-called "Craft Magic" and joyously embrace schooling.

"We are all as the Goddess made us," he whispered, and smiled thinly. It was a thing his master had been prone to say; the comfortable mantra of a man comfortable in his faith. Goddess thanked he had not lived to see this.

He looked again at the proclamation, at the unweathered parchment, the crisp ribbons, and the bright nail holding it to the wall over the owl's left wing. Posted new this morn, or so he judged it.

There was a guildhall in the city. A very full guildhall, no doubt, this being Beltane and practitioners of the "Craft Magic" standing at least as devout as the rest of the populace. On average.

Behind him, he heard steps—voices bearing down toward the merry red door. In that instant, he made his decision, flicked a hand out, then melted into the shadows aside the doorway. The two customers—younger sons of outer ring market families, by their dress and accent—passed within a finger's breadth and never saw him.

The door swung closed and Lute stepped into the street, moving with long, unhurried strides—back toward the deep of the city.

Behind him, the carven owl stood vigil over sign, door and a bright, new nail.

THE HIGH PRIESTESS

Wisdom, serenity, judgment, learning, sagacity, common sense

"Lady Moonhawk! Lady Moonhawk, come quickly!" The novice who demanded it hurtled pell-mell into the library, sandals grating on the polished wooden floor. She hit one of the red and yellow rugs with no diminishment of speed, skidded—and would have fallen except that the woman curled in the window glanced up from her book and prevented it with a flicker of long fingers and the breath of a Word.

"Thank you, Lady!" the novice gasped, belatedly recalling her bow. She performed this ritual hurriedly, straightened without having received the Lady's aye and blurted again: "You must come quickly!"

Lady Moonhawk lifted an eyebrow, dark blue eyes sharpening on the novice's face. "Oh," she said, in dangerously sweet accents, "Must I?"

The novice gulped, nervously tangling her fingers together before her. "Please, Lady, it's—"

"Keela's baby." Moonhawk was up in the same instant, moving with long strides across the slippery floor. "Fetch Mother Portal," she snapped over her shoulder as she vanished into the hallway.

"Yes, Lady Moonhawk," the novice said and quit the room herself, forbearing to run until she hit the stone-floored hallway.

#

It had been a hard birth and the baby had not been hale, so both mother and child had been brought to the Temple Infirmary, to be cared for by the Circle until both were strong.

Keela did well, gaining weight and strength with joyous ease. The babe had not done as well, though neither Moonhawk nor any of the other Healing Sisters could determine what it was that ailed him.

"He has no will to live," Greenlady had said, though not in the mother's hearing. "Poor babe, he hangs by a thread, as if life were a fault in the weaving, rather than the purpose of the loom."

There was wisdom in that, Moonhawk thought, for the boy certainly showed no spark of the all-consuming interest characteristic of other children his age. She probed him, seeking his soul, seeking the nature of his mind—and found only weariness, as one might find when aiding those full old to prepare for their reunion with the Goddess.

Just as well, she thought, that he return to the Mother now. . .

Aye, the next thought intruded, and what of Keela?

Keela, who had lost her man this winter past, when the river ice cracked wide and the frigid waters dragged him down; who had rejoiced in a son to bear his likeness—and his name. Keela, who nursed the sickly boy with fierce patience, holding him in her arms, willing him to life with a potency that bordered upon a Sister's skill.

What of Keela, should the child die, too?

Moonhawk began to run.

#

The Infirmary was quiet as she dashed into the common room, so that she dared hope—and then she saw Keela, bent over the cradle, her arms moving in the way Moonhawk had taught her. She was pressing on the child's chest, helping him breathe.

Moonhawk stopped at the cradle's side, watching Keela work, caught a whiff of the other woman's desperate terror, saw the thin chest rise and fall under his mother's hands.

"He breathes," she said. "Keela, let him take it up."

"He breathes," Keela said grimly. "Three times before I thought so, and when I stopped, he did as well!" She glanced aside, face grim and wet with sweat. "Lady Moonhawk, my child is dying!"

It seared of Truth. Moonhawk opened herself to the trance, stepping into it even as she stepped forward and put her hand beside the other woman's hand, upon the baby's breast.

"Let me See," she said and then she said no more, nor saw more, either, except what lay before the Inner Eyes.

A wasteland lay stretched before her, parched, misbegotten and doomed. There was no air, nor sun, no water, no joy.

In the world she had left, Moonhawk's other hand moved to rest atop Keela's own.

A second landscape overlay the first, this one lush with life and love and joy, save that where it crossed the wastland, patches of lush greenery became tainted; here and there strands of grass were seen to die.

And as the two landscapes stretched further together, each bound into the other, the first began to leach more life from the second, killing wholesale, until, on the edge of the horizon, Moonhawk could see no difference between them—only deserted waste, stretching onward forever.

Chilled, she closed the Inner Eyes, took one glimpse at the mother's grim desperation, moved both her hands and lifted Keela away from the child.

"No!" One cry, anguished, and Keela slumped against her, face hidden against Moonhawk's shoulder. Moonhawk held her close, stroking the disordered hair, opened the Inner Eyes—and Watched the baby die.

It came quickly—only a fading, a shuddering sigh of ultimate easement, with no need of her to smooth the path, without a note of the singing joy so commonly heard at the last instant. Joyless alive, joyless he died, giving up the life that had been only burden.

"Gone," she said and felt Keela shudder, then move away. The Inner Vision spun for a heartbeat, then steadied, showing again the exuberant land that was Keela, showing a small near patch of blight, then a lush regrowth. The sun was warm, and Moonhawk thought she heard birdsong.

She opened her eyes.

Keela was holding her son in her arms, tears running her face, breast heaving. "The Goddess gives," she gasped, half-raising her face.

"And the Goddess receives us back," murmured a soft voice from beside Moonhawk.

"Lady Portal."

The Mother of Dyan Circle bowed slightly. "I see I am too late." She lay a tiny hand upon Moonhawk's sleeve. "Come to me after Tenth Chant."

"Yes, Mother." Dismissed, Moonhawk bowed deeply and turned away. Mother Portal's soft voice followed her out of the room, accompanied by the first subtle flavors of a Heart Heal: "There, there, my child. Come, lay the lad down in his crib. No, there's no shame in crying. Such a bonny boy he was and so strongly did you fight for him. . ."

Except, Moonhawk thought, she'd lost, despite the love and the fight, and the combined efforts of three Witches skilled in healing. In the end, the babe *would* die, and perhaps better he had never lived at all. She caught her lower lip in her teeth at such a thought and turned her mind forcibly to the prayers to establish serenity.

#

She returned to her own rooms, bathed and dressed in a fresh gown of the shade known outside Temple as "Circle blue," and cut to fully reveal the breasts.

Any other of the Sisters would then have repaired to the Lady's Chapel in Temple's center or to the private altar each kept within her room, to meditate on events just past, to seek portents and signs of things left undone for the soul returned, to achieve communion with the Power that moved the universe.

Moonhawk went to the East Tower.

There, she stared into the late day sky, and when the hawk spiraled into sight, she brought her arm up, crooked so, as if this were a tame beast and not wild the length and breadth of its days.

She held her arm up and, obedient, the hawk stooped, cruel talons digging tight into the invisible shield she conjured to protect her fragile flesh.

The invisible shield was a small magic, in Moonhawk's estimation. The miracle was having one of the Goddess' wildest children with her of its free feral will, looking without fear into her eyes.

They stayed so, Witch and hawk, for a timeless time, staring deeply into each other's eyes, drinking each of the soul of the other. Then the woman moved, slowly bringing up her other hand, and trailed her fingers through the chest feathers in caress.

The bird allowed it: One stroke, from chin to belly, then it flicked its wings, and broke the gaze that had bound both.

Obedient in her turn, Moonhawk brought her arm sharply up and the bird was gone in a blast of wings, soaring upward into the purpling twilight, until it was lost to the Witch's straining eyes.

Regretfully, she brought her eyes down, bent and picked up the barred brown feather from between her bare feet. "Thank you," she murmured, and moved to the parapet.

One hip braced against the low wall, she gazed down into Goddess Square as her fingers seperated a lock of hair and began to make a braid into which the hawk's feather would be woven.

Pilgrims had been flowing in for the past half-moon, two, three, a dozen every day, and now, on the evening before Beltane, it would seem that all had gained the security of the Supplicant's Courtyard. The plaza she gazed down on was empty, except for those townfolk who crossed it in the course of normal business. At the foot of Maidenstairs there was no one, travel-stained and weary, come down from the mountains to partake of Beltane at the Temple, to offer themselves up to the Spring Goddess and beg for good growth, good fortune, good health.

But no, what was this? From the ring streets came a man, dark-cloaked and dark-haired, barely more than a blot against the shadowing air, striding purposefully toward Maidenstairs.

Straight across the plaza he came, looking neither right nor left, eyes seemingly fixed on Maidenstairs. He moved with long graceful strides, but Moonhawk caught a sense of weariness rise up from him, as if he had kept the pace for longer than was wise.

At the foot of Maidenstairs, he stopped, cloak swinging into stillness, embracing him with shadow.

The First Hound was barely around the edge of the tower where she leaned, braiding the feather into her hair; the supplicant had time, just, to climb the stairs and beg Sister Doorkeeper the boon of shelter and food for the night.

He remained quite, quite still, as if having come this far his resolve now failed him. Moonhawk leaned more nearly over the parapet, heedless of the dangers of overbalance, and sought him with the Inner Eyes. If she could but discover the fading ember of courage, entice it to flame once more...

Weariness she read in him, as clearly as if he were a Sister in Circle; hunger, and a spark of honest anger, overridden at once by wariness. Moonhawk blinked, very nearly overbalanced at Center by the clarity with which he could be read. Yet, she Saw no trace of that which must have carried him many days and miles.

Biting her lip, she embraced the prayer for serenity and prepared herself to attempt a deeper Reading.

The man in the plaza below moved.

Gracefully, he sank to one knee, sleek head bent in respect.

Three heartbeats later, he came as gracefully to his feet, and backed nine smoothly precise steps away from Maidenstairs, his shadowed face lifted to the East Tower. If it had been day, Moonhawk thought, he might have seen her; she might have been able somehow to influence him to mount the stairs, and enter the comfort and safety—

The man turned away, walking back across Goddess Square, his stride still smooth, though less long, less—driven.

Moonhawk watched until he vanished into the shadows of the ring-street, unaccountably troubled by his failure. So small a thing, to climb Maidenstairs, to ask the ritual question and be welcomed within. So small a price to pay for relief of whatever had driven him so wearily. To lose a soul from one instant of human fraility—

She shook her head, smiling wryly. Peace, Lady Moonhawk, she told herself. Well you know that no soul is ever lost. The Goddess speaks to us all in the tongue we know best. Yon seeker this time heard imperfectly. Next time he'll doubtless hear fully.

Doubtless. She raised her face to the Hound and stretched both hands high, palms open, naked feet braced against the tower stones, welcoming the weak power of the lesser moon into her, letting it wash away her grief for the dead child, the lost seeker, allowing her soul to take wing and soar as the hawk had soared, spriralling gloriously upward.

The bell-notes preceding Ninth Chant brought her to herself with a gasp and she lowered stiffened arms. The Hound was behind her, half-done its first circuit of the night. The Moon itself would rise at Twelfth Chant, at which time the Founding Ritual that prepared all for Beltane itself, would take over the attention of the Circle. Goddess Plaza, deserted now below her, would be crowded with townspeople eager to lend their energy and good heart to the ritual.

Her talk with Mother Portal would be over by then, and she would be with the others in the center courtyard, raising her voice with them in the opening songs, merging her being with the beings of her Sisters, raising and sustaining power—the first complex level of power needed for the coming joyous ritual. . .

She should, she thought abruptly, eat something. In general she was careless of meals, but the hunger she had tasted of the seeker nagged at the pit of her own stomach. Food, she thought, firmly, and so thinking climbed down from the tower and went down the long hallways to the kitchen.

When she arrived there, she made a good meal of roast lamb and spiced vegetables and fresh bread with sweet butter. She ate methodically, and more than she would have eaten for herself, as if she might feed the unknown seeker, too.

#

"And so you felt it time to allow Keela's baby his death?" The question was mild, as all of Mother Portal's questions were mild, but Moonhawk felt a chill pebble her skin.

"With the Inner Eyes I Saw how it was with the babe, how he would take all of Keela's joy and remain joyless. How, if he were to return to the Goddess, she would heal, and he would have the Summerland, and rest before his next incarnation. It was True Seeing." She heard the defensive note in her own voice, bit her lip and moved her eyes to contemplate the green-and-silver candle burning upon Lady Portal's private altar.

"True Seeing." The tone was bland, empty of any compulsion or command. "But not Goddess-moved."

Moonhawk turned her head to stare at her interrogator. "Goddess-moved?" she echoed. "No, Mother. It was myself who Saw, who knew right action and acted."

"So," Mother Portal said. "Lady Moonhawk takes it upon herself to judge who should live and whose life is a burden no longer to be borne."

"It is what the Inner Eyes are for!" Moonhawk cried. "It is what I was trained for, why I was shown to the Goddess and taught the Inner Magics—"

"And you believe that attaining the Inner Circle makes you like unto the Goddess, able to give life and take it?" Sharp as ice now, Lady Portal's voice, and each small cold cut hurt and bewildered, so that Moonhawk sat back upon her heels and merely stared.

"Answer," Lady Portal directed and Moonhawk licked her lips.

"Mother, I have told you what I Saw. I believe that I acted rightly, in accordance with the Way I was shown and with the Will of the Goddess as I have been taught to understand it. It is my private belief that the child wished to die and that as he grew older his wish would grow greater until it would have taken all the Circle, concentrating all their energy upon him and him alone to keep him from the Summerland."

"And so you acted and took away the hands that might have saved him one more time and allowed him to slip away now." There was a pause during which Moonhawk ran through an exercise to embrace Serenity and abandoned herself to the will of the Goddess.

"How do you know," demanded Lady Portal, "that it was *time* for that child to die, Lady Moonhawk? Did your True Seeing show you that?"

Within the warming cloak of Serenity, Moonhawk felt a spear-thrust of ice pierce straight to her heart.

"No," she murmured. "I did not know that."

"So." Lady Portal stared at her, eyes showing sadness. "I have had reports from others of our Sisters," she said slowly. "They tell me that Lady Moonhawk is full with herself, that, though her talents are great, so is her pride. That Lady Moonhawk alone is the best judge of ritual rightly done, of results correctly obtained." She glanced down at her hands, folded upon her lap; looked up again into Moonhawk's face.

"How long have you been in Circle, Sister?"

"How long—" Moonhawk caught herself staring again; blinked. "All my life, Mother," she said carefully. "I was brought here as an infant, to fulfill my birth-mother's vow to the Lady."

"And, showing talent as soon as you could walk, you were trained, knowledge poured into you until you were full to bursting and with a flick of your fingers can conjure a spell that another of our Sisters, less talented, yet industrious and good-hearted, may spend days of careful ritual to achieve." She closed her eyes.

Moonhawk sought again the green-and-silver candle, and abandoned both thought and unease. It would transpire as the Goddess willed it, she thought firmly, pulling the rags of Serenity about her. Whatever punishment might be hers, for failing to read fully, that she would do. Neither Mother Portal nor her Sisters in Circle nor the Goddess would put upon her more than she might bear.

Mother Portal opened her eyes. "You are arrogant," she said slowly, each word a pebble, dropped into the still pool of Moonhawk's mind. "Further, you are ignorant. It is our duty, who have trained you, to see that these faults in you are amended, so that you may serve the Goddess to the full extent of your powers. I shall meditate upon it, as shall the Circle." She moved, rising to her full, diminutive height, and smoothed her hands down the front of her rumpled robe. Moonhawk rose as well and stood looking down at her, Serenity yet cloaking thoughts and emotions.

"You will go to your rooms," Mother Portal said. "You will cleanse yourself and you will do a Crossing Over ritual for Keela's child. You will then fast and meditate and await my call."

Within Serenity, a spark of panic. "But—Beltane. . ."

Lady Portal looked severe. "Beltane was before there was Moonhawk," she said sternly. "And Beltane there will be long after Moonhawk is returned to the Goddess. Do not add disobedience to your transgressions."

Moonhawk stood, and stared.

Lady Portal sighed. "You have your instructions, I believe?" she said, voice unremittingly even.

The panic had gone from spark to conflagration, through which that dangerously mild tone cut like a honed blade. Moonhawk bowed low—"Yes, Mother. Blessed be."—and left the room.

Numb, she walked down halls glowing with the lambent energy of nearly a hundred excited Witches and novices. She was bumped once or twice by those hurrying toward Moon Court for the midnight ritual, but most of the tide she moved against avoided her scrupulously. No one called her name in friendship. No one caught her sleeve and laughingly scolded her for walking the wrong way. She moved alone, as she ever did, through halls crowded with the Sisters of her Circle.

It wasn't until she reached her own room, the door closed and sealed behind her, that she released Serenity and began to cry.

The Ace of Pentacles

The beginning and the end

The Moon had risen since he had quit Goddess Square, and the access streets were crowded with those who wished to partake of the foundation rituals performed on Beltane eve.

The devout made a river of humanity, carrying Lute toward Dyan Temple and the living heart of the city.

A human river, however, could be fought as a Goddess-sent compulsion could not. Lute used shoulders and elbows to steer himself through and across the current, to land at last, ill-tempered and sweaty, at the door of the Magician's Guildhall.

It was locked.

Lute stared for a long moment, bag heavy across his shoulder, then grabbed the bell-rope and pulled. The door remained shut.

"Damn you," he gritted and renewed his grip on the rope. Over and over, he hauled down, waking such a peal that his head fair rang with it—and at long last the door came open a cautious inch.

"Go away," snarled someone from within. "It's Beltane eve."

Lute glared into the dark as if he could see the speaker well. "Tell the Guildmaster that Master Magician Lute is here to speak to him upon a matter of utmost urgency."

"Be silent, or are you Moonkissed?" The keeper would have shut the door then, except that Lute's foot prevented it. "Maiden's tits, man, will you have us all called to Circle? It's Beltane. Go away."

"It is most certainly Beltane eve, and I will just as certainly not go away." Lute snapped. "I will see the Master of this Hall if I have to ring the bell until the roof falls in! Let me in—my right as Guildsman!—and fetch the Master." He paused for the beat of two, called up the voice-power as his master had taught him and released it in one word: "*Now*."

It worked. It nearly always did work, even against those who knew the trick of it. The doorkeeper sagged back a step, the door widened an inch more, Lute got his shoulder into the gap and shoved.

A half-beat later he was standing in the dim entrance way, closing the door behind him over the keeper's sputtering, and scrupulously lowering the bar. He fixed the older man with a stern eye.

"Fetch the Guildmaster."

"He's not here," said the keeper, sullenly. "Nor should you be, if you have a taste for health."

Lute lifted a brow, magnificently ignoring the man's surliness. "If the Guildmaster if not here," he said, keeping his voice sweet, "then send for him."

"But—"

"And after you've done that," he continued, brooking no debate. "You will show me to a parlor and bring me the latest log books, and a sup of ale. And some cheese. That is all."

The doorkeeper gaped at him, so Lute was forced to clap his hands sharply and flick the voice-lash: "*Go*!

"Yes, Master," muttered the servant, startled into a bow. He scuttled off down the hallway, leaving Lute in dimness. Sighing, he walked to the wall, noting the position of the three ready sconces—set well above his overlong reach, a silly place, really, for torches, unless one wished to make a point.

He backed away from the wall, counting his steps, then, exactly centered upon one of the fine-cut granite blocks flooring the hallway, he stamped his heel three times, cried "Ho!" and flung his arms high, fingers stretched wide, miming the flames that leapt instantly in all three sconces at once.

Slowly, he lowered his arms, keeping his face as solemn as if there were a crowd to impress, and as if satisfaction did not soar in him, that he had not lost the trick of it.

"Master's work," commented a voice to his right, abruptly enough to intend to startle. Lute finished the gesture properly, allowed his cloak to wrap him in mysterious stillness and held it for one long beat before he turned to face his audience.

"How pleasant to hear you say so," he purred and had the satisfaction of seeing the man's jowly face take on a pinkish tinge. He bowed, sweeping the cloak out and making it seem of velvet and ermine, to thus place it on a level with his host's 'broidered scarlet sash and silken shirt.

He of the scarlet sash bowed also, with grace, but without wit. "I am Feldris, newly Master of Dyan City Magician's Hall."

"And I am Lute, Master Magician, who had been apprentice of Master Magician Cereus."

"Registered of what Hall?" The question was an insult; the names of all Master Magicians were inscribed in the *Book of Masters* kept in each Guildhall and it was the duty of each Hallkeeper to have that Book by heart. Lute lifted an eyebrow.

"Hagsmere, and it please you, great lord."

Feldris colored again, mouth tightening ominously. "I regret," he said stiffly, "that I am new to the house and have not committed the names of all the Masters to memory."

"A failing deserving of regret," Lute acknowledged, around a sudden sense of foreboding. "Let us step over to the Common Room and pull down the register, that you may satisfy yourself of my—authenticity."

The other man fluttered his hands—a formless thing, and thoroughly unlike the measured gesture one expected from a brother magician. Lute felt his foreboding grow, the parchment in his sleeve as heavy as stone.

"I am certain you are who—and what—you say you are," Feldris Hallkeeper said soothingly. "Did I not with my own eyes see you light the torches? But the doorkeeper spoke of an urgent matter you must discuss, and I have kept you waiting long enough. In what way can Dyan Guildhall aid you?"

Foreboding flared into active dismay. Here? Lute wondered, keeping his face bland. In the very entrance hall? With neither table nor greet-wine nor the witness of others of the Guild?

"It is a matter of sufficient import," he murmured, "to interest all currently resident within the hall."

"Ah." Feldris folded his unschooled hands before his sash. "That would be myself," he said. "And the doorkeeper, of course."

"Is everyone at the Foundation Rituals, then?"

"They are no longer in the city," the Guildmaster said softly.

Lute took a breath, and then another. "Well," he said lightly, "I can see that I've wasted my time and yours, sir! Good Beltane to you—" He turned smoothly and went, smoothly, toward the door, ignoring his stammering heart and the lungs that wished to labor.

"Hold!" The Guildmaster's tread was heavy behind him and Lute was too far from the door—fool that he had been to bar it!

"Hold!" Feldris cried again as Lute laid his hands upon the bar and—

"Hold!"

"Hold!"

"*Hold!*"

Cried three separate voices from three corners of the entrance way, so that Feldris spun on his heel, surprised by words in the hall he knew to be empty. Lute flung the bar aside with a clatter, jerked the door wide—

And ran.

#

To become invisible it is merely necessary to become one of many.

Thus had his master had taught him, and good lore it was, as far as it walked. It was certainly no failing on the part of Master Cereus that his apprentice wished most ardently to avoid the place where the shielding crowd was thickest.

"If I wanted congress with Circle, I could as easily have clung to Master Feldris' side."

So saying, Lute left the crowd two streets short of Goddess Square and ducked into the shadow of an ornate garden gate, there to complete his preparations in private.

Master Cereus had been a gentle man, but no one's fool. He had walked a rough road for upwards of forty years and took no lasting harm from it. It had been his ardent wish that his 'prentice did as well.

"Of course," Lute muttered to himself in the privacy of the gate-shadow, "he never meant you to fight Circle, either. Each as the Goddess made us, master. Excepting only that the Goddess has lately reached forth her hand and made some of us more perfect than others."

He freed his bag from its carrying strap and knelt by it on the paving stones, hands hasty on the secret clasps. In the very act of unsealing it, he stopped, hands gripping the worn black leather.

The Guildhall where he—three times a fool!—ignored the gatekeeper's most obvious warning. And Feldris—no magician he, nor even one who had much experience of the breed, to be so startled by a minor bit of ventriloquism. Newly come to the post, was he, by Moon? And by whose aye, with the Guildhall empty and Dyan City's magicians "gone?" Lute sat back on his heels and shivered as might-have-been ran down his back on many cold feet.

Feldris might well follow him: For his own safety, Lute must suppose that the hunt was already on. However, the pretty sash and soft hands spoke of one not so familiar with the rough, twisty streets along the city's outer ring. It was in those streets that Lute intended to pass the night, and be out the Western Gate the moment it opened, tomorrow.

"Fortunate, indeed, if dawn sees you out of the city," he told himself grimly. "Remember this and never again go within gates."

He took a deep breath then, and performed the linked series of mental images that had been the first magic his master had taught him. Calmed by the exercise, hands steady and mind cool, he finished the necessary adjustments to the bag.

A moment later he was out on the street, joining the crowd running there, and let it bear him, resistless, toward Goddess Square and the choice of multiple routes to the outer city.

#

Some time later he was moving toward a spur street tending westward and out and feeling a bit more sanguine regarding his chances of winning clear. So he ambled along, angling through the crowd, the picture of a man vaguely questing—for a lover, perhaps, or an aged parent—nothing frantic, to draw the eye, nor even particularly purposeful.

Inside the cloak, he rounded his shoulders to disguise his height and took care to walk heavy on the paving stones, to foster the illusion of bulk.

It took time to do the thing thus, but he judged it to his advantage to allow time for his path to grow cold to the nose of whatever hounds the false Guildmaster might call out to the chase.

So he thought and so he believed. And so did this endeavor appear to have the Mother's smile, for he had the proper street in his eye; and was beginning to count the steps until he began once more to be safe—when he of the 'broidered sash, Master Feldris himself, stepped out of the street that Lute had thought his salvation, stopped and looked directly into the magician's eyes.

His jowly face lit as if he'd been chosen for Temple consort, flushing pink as he pointed at the place where Lute had been and looked over his shoulder to call out, "Here he is, Lady! Come quickly!"

But whether the lady obeyed such ungenteel summons or not, Lute could not have said. He was running, pushing and shoving and not caring whose feet he trod on—running, back into the thickest of the crowd.

THE FOOL

Simplicity, Faith

Upon her balcony overlooking the innermost garden, Moonhawk sat in meditation. Outer eyes closed, she yet saw the greening bushes, the budding trees and the soft new grass with exquisite clarity. The garden was a haven of tranquility, after all, and many potent spells had been woven to insure that tranquility. It was a fitting model for the meditations of one judged by her sisters to be hasty and arrogant.

It had taken work to shed her bitterness at being excluded from Beltane eve circle; work that, in her current meek state, only illustrated more painfully that she was not fit for Inner Circle; and much less than fit for her duty as vessel of the Goddess.

With these realizations newly in hand, she had eschewed the more sophisticated trance-patterns and opted for one that needed no drawn-out ritual to birth it, but merely required her own unimpaired Sight, and a relaxing of her arrogant will.

Upon the balcony, deep in meditation, Moonhawk *was* the garden and the peace therein.

Until, in the garden, there was—discord.

It was a slight thing, quickly gone, but it was enough to pain her, linked as she was—more than enough to break the web of trance.

Eyes still closed, but alert now, and seeking, Moonhawk cast her net out to capture the cause of discord.

She found it nearly at once: A pattern startling in its clarity, tinged with elusive familiarity. From the surface thoughts she caught frustration and anger, desperation, yet not despair. She received the impression that the intruder was being hunted, without expectation of either mercy or succor.

Hunted, on Beltane! Moonhawk stood, and opened her outer eyes, coordinating what she saw with what her other senses brought her. She established the intruder's location and nodded.

Hunted, in the very garden of the Inmost Circle!

Moonhawk went to the edge of the balcony, stepped off and walked the air down to the ground.

Feet upon the path, she paused once more to be certain of her direction, then set off at a rapid walk.

#

He had been a fool to think that the hounds Feldris would bring to the hunt could be any less than Witches.

Not one Witch, as he had first thought, but *three*. Almost, he laughed. Three Witches and a false Guildmaster to run one ragged conjurer to ground? Soberness claimed him in a chill rush. Was *this* the reason the Goddess had herded him to Dyan City? That he might be held as an example to others of his profession?

Yet, for whatever reasons, three Witches. More than enough to push him in the direction they chose, and to deny him any hope of the streets beyond the square.

What they had aimed for, he thought, was to pin him against the base of East Tower, there to gather him up at their leisure. But he had moved a little too quickly; played the crowd-currents a little too adeptly. He came to the wall near the tower, certainly, but to the north, hard by the wicket he had noted earlier in the evening. It was the work of a moment to pick the lock and slip through, and hardly more than that to make sure the gate was locked again behind him.

He doubted his ploy would hold his pursuers long, but he hoped it would hold them long enough for him to hide himself. For in all the great pile of Dyan Temple, he thought, treading the conch-lined path with care, there must be one small hole into which he might crawl, there to sleep through Beltane. He would let himself out the way he had come in tomorrow.

The path made a sharp turn and twisted through a taelberry arbor, turned again. . .

And ended at a blank wall.

The wall must protect a private garden, Lute thought, refusing to accede to despair. The private garden, perhaps, of some Witch, who, if she held rank high enough to possess such a quiet spot, might well be a part of the Beltane eve rituals taking place in the Moon Court even now.

Beltane itself did not come to fruition until Moonrise tomorrow and there were certain other rituals after, so he had heard, that might keep a ranking lady well away from her garden.

It was the best gamble he had, who should have quit the table long ago. He brought gloves from beneath his cloak and pulled them on before he set his hands carefully among the wallstones and began to climb.

The wall was admirably supplied with hand- and foot-holds. Moments later Lute dropped lightly to the floor of the garden beyond, stripped off his gloves and headed for the shalmon bush at the base of the cort tree. He slipped in tight against the trunk, cloak melding with the black bark. The bush clothed him with leaf to the knee.

He leaned his forehead against the tree and deliberately emptied his mind of everything that was Lute or of Lute's concerns. He was a part of the garden, just quickening with spring. He was the cort tree, warm, smooth bark, widespread branches, soft, feathery leaves.

And then he was nothing, merely a blot of shadow among the other shadows beneath the tree. Invisible, not there, never there, safe and calm and—

"It is you!"

The voice shattered his self-hypnosis and he jumped; stumbled within the embrace of the shalmon bush, and would have fallen except that strong hands caught his shoulders and held him gently upright.

"It *is* you," the voice reiterated. "But however did you come here?"

The speaker was nearly his own height; yellow-haired and angular, dressed in the blue, breast-baring robe of an Initiate. Lute felt his heart go to ice.

As if she felt his dread, the woman held out a slim hand and stepped away from his hiding place. Rings of power glittered in the moonlight—enough silver to feed him for a goodly number of years, baring an unnaturally short life.

"Come," the woman said gently, "you don't need to be afraid. No harm will come to you here, I swear it!" She moved her fingers, beckoning, as if he were a bashful child.

"Come," she said again, and he stepped out of the bush and went two steps toward her across the grass. He could think of no place, now, to run.

"Good," said the woman—the *Witch*. "I saw you earlier, at the base of Maidenstairs; I was sorry you had not come in. But you are here now and may find peace, for the Goddess is Mother of us all and Her Temples are safe havens for all Her children." She tipped her head.

"You are still afraid, but you needn't be. No one will hurt you here. Haven't I said so?"

"There he is!" He heard the words and felt the blow at the same time: A blow as from a giant's fist, slamming into his skull, driving him to one knee as the world shimmered and started to go gray. . .

"No! I have said he is safe here!" The world steadied and took back its colors; the pain in his head receded to a dull ache. Lute looked up, saw Feldris and another woman in Circle blue coming toward himself and his champion. This woman was smaller, rounder, darker, and frowning like a thunderhead.

"*You* have said he's safe here," she snapped. "And what have you to do with it?"

The yellow-haired Witch pulled herself up. "He failed at the door at First Hound—I saw it! Now, he comes to us, but afraid. Afraid of being hunted, Sister! Remind me, is it not Beltane eve?"

The dark one lifted a brow. "You know very well the name of the ceremony from which you are excluded."

"Yes?" the taller woman said with a false sweetness that set Lute's teeth on edge. "And yourself?"

"You—*dare*! On what day and hour was Moonhawk named Circle's Center? *I* draw my duties from the Circle, and to the Circle alone do I explain my reasons!"

"Strange," murmured Lute, climbing to his feet and wincing at the persisting headache, "I'd have thought you might reserve time for that which the Goddess sends you."

"Be silent!" snapped the dark woman, tracing a sharp sign before her. Lute saw the image shine against the air for an instant, then vanish.

"Certainly," he said and bowed, slightly and with irony. "Since you ask it so nicely."

The dark woman fairly gaped, but her escort was at no loss of words.

"Respect for Lady Rowan!" he cried and came two strides forward, fist rising. Lute watched his approach calmly; saw him stop as if suddenly rooted as the tall Witch wove her hand through glittering air.

"Shame, Feldris Circleman! To move for violence within these walls!"

Feldris Circleman. Lute stared at the other, searching the soft face and haughty eyes. A servant of the Temple, perhaps even the angry lady's consort. Thus might Lute have been. . .

"This man," Lady Rowan was telling—Moonhawk?—pointing at Lute's very self, "is a breaker of the peace and one who actively works to rend Circle and lead the ignorant into error. He must be brought before Truth-seers at once."

Lute stirred. "I am of course honored that word of my skill has come to the ears of the ladies of Dyan Circle," he said smoothly. "However, I have traveled hard the last few days and doubt not my work is grown ragged." He smiled, noting how Lady Rowan's eyes sparked with fury even as her cheeks seemed to pale.

"I would bring nothing less than my best performance," he said gently, "before your sisters."

Lady Rowan walked forward, heavy, deliberate steps that crushed the new grass beneath her bare feet. Straight past Feldris Circleman she went until she stood less than an arm's length from Lute and there stopped, looking up at him with her hands on her hips.

"I bade you be silent. *Magician*."

Lute felt a spark of anger, though he kept his face pleasant. Make a curse-word of his profession, would she? He bowed once again, slight and mocking.

"Why so you did," he said, smiling down at her. "Forgive me a faulty memory."

Her lips tightened, and she brought her hands sharply up, tracing a design that shone like living bars of fire in the air between them. He heard the other woman make a small sound even as his tongue began to burn.

Never anger a Witch, he thought as the pain grew and he felt the roof of his mouth scalding. The inside of his cheeks began to fry and he wanted, desperately, to scream—

"Avert!" One word, that seemed to lance through his tortured mouth like a spear of ice. The pain died on the instant and Lute closed his eyes in blessed relief. He opened them again to see Lady Rowan turning toward Moonhawk.

"You will cease to meddle! You will free my servant and return to your meditations. When Mother Portal hears of this—"

"Which she will better hear from my lips than yours, I think, Sister," said Moonhawk coolly. "Let us go together, why not?"

"Together?" Lady Rowan had gone very still.

"Together," Moonhawk replied, looking down upon her. "Where should this man better go than to Mother Portal, who knows Truth as plain as any other Seer?" She smiled, but not warmly. "And how better to bring word of my trespass most quickly to her ear?"

There was a hard silence, then a nod. "Very well," said Lady Rowan stiffly. "Join with me in subduing the magician—"

"Subduing?" Lute felt Moonhawk's glance like a physical thing. "He hardly seems frantic, though he has every right to be. Few folk, you know, Sister, would stand calm while their tongue was set afire."

"Oh," said Lady Rowan, ignoring the rebuke. "So you think he'll come quiet, do you?"

"Why should he not?" returned Moonhawk, then lifted her shoulders in a shrug. "But, there, you're distraught yourself and hard-ly in condition to lend support. I'll lead him and there will be no trouble." Another thoughtful blue glance at his face. "Will there, Master Lute?"

His name, which he had not told her. He stared, speechless now that he was required to speak, then drew himself up, conjuring a grin. "No trouble at all, Lady. My word upon it."

#

Mother Portal's rooms were hung with silvery tapestries, upholstered in velvets and furs. Green and silver candles burned at the four prime points—green for the Spring Goddess, silver for the Moon. A fat white cat with a green riband about his neck sprawled across a low round table inlaid with gemstones. Incense hung in a pall, overbur-dening the air with the scent of false roses, and the windows were shut tight against the fine spring night.

"Take off your cloak," Lady Rowan snapped and Lute froze, eyes going to his patroness.

Moonhawk returned his glance gravely. "You've no need of your cloak here, Master Lute. The room is warm. And it is discourteous to come covered before Mother Portal."

"Ah," he said, around the dread in his heart. "Moon knows I would not be churlish."

He raised his hand and twisted the copper brooch at his shoul-der, let the cloak slip free and caught it up in a practiced motion that never brought the lining to sight. Feldris Circleman had it off of his arm the next instant, and Lute bit back a protest.

"He's only gone to hang it up," said Moonhawk. "You shall have it again when you go."

"Yes," said Lute gently, for she seemed out of reason young and touchingly certain of his eventual freedom. "Of course I shall."

Lady Rowan was a different matter. "That!" she snapped, pointing at the bag, suspended from its leather strap and hanging at his hip. "Give that to me!"

It was the command voice again. Lute stilled the involuntary move of his muscles to obey, took three deep breaths and looked into Lady Rowan's eyes.

"No."

Her breath hissed. "You—*charlatan*! Have a care what enemies you make, lest you buy above your means." She snapped her fingers. "Give me the bag."

"No."

"And why should he?" Moonhawk demanded, cutting through whatever new pain Lady Rowan was doubtless contemplating inflicting upon him. "It is his, after all."

"It is proof of his villainy and it shall be set out now, ready for Lady Portal's hand."

"It is my life and my livelihood," Lute cried, anger breaking its barriers for an instant. "Nor is it safe for Lady Portal or any other except myself to touch it!"

"That is True," said Moonhawk into the small silence that followed this outburst. "He believes what he has said, completely."

There was more silence, then a flicker of Lady Rowan's fingers. "Show him the logic of putting it aside, Sister, do," she said, but to Lute's ear it sounded more an order than a request. "If the thing is as dangerous as that and he the only one who may control it, we can hardly take the chance of him unchaining it and making good his escape."

"Escape." Once more those blue eyes rested fully on him. "Do you wish to escape us, Master Lute?"

"Yes," he told her with utter truth.

She frowned. "I am sorry to hear it," she said gravely, "but I can scarcely blame you. Rough treatment has been your share here thus far. Still, Lady Rowan speaks sensibly, you know. If your bag is as dangerous as you believe, with yourself distressed and likely to err, perhaps it would be best for all, if you simply put the strap off and set the bag here." She pointed to a place upon the costly carpet exactly halfway between them. "Is that an acceptable compromise?"

He stared at the spot where her finger pointed, felt the weight of the bag across his shoulder, and thought, briefly and wildly, of the mountain village he had quit nine days ago, when the compulsion had come upon him—

"Lady," he said, seeking Moonhawk's glance, willing her to see the Truth in him. "I have no more will to break Circle than that cat!"

She held his eyes for a long moment, until Lute felt himself sliding into light-headedness, then glanced aside, a tiny line between her brows.

"But you know," she said in her grave deep voice, "that is not *quite* true, Master Lute." She moved her hand, showing him the spot on the carpet once more. "The bag here, if you please."

There was no help for it. With a flourish he slid the strap free, leaned forward and placed his bag precisely upon the designated place, face betraying none of the profound dismay in his heart.

"Thank you," said Moonhawk. "I will see that none harm it, Master Lute. I say so before the Goddess."

"Fine promises," mocked Lady Rowan and Moonhawk spun quick, eyes flashing and lips parting for a scorching reply, so Lute was certain. But—

"Enough!" cried a new voice, accompanied by the sharp sound of a clap. "Can I not be out of my rooms for an hour without returning to find two Sisters squabbling like brats?"

The lady who demanded it wore a shawl across her bony shoulders, and her fine Circle robe was rumpled as if she had passed many nights in it. Her hair was gray, with a bluish cast to it, snarled as if she had been out in the wind. Overall, she was tiny—small on height and short on meat, as the country folk told it—and her face was rodent-sharp, dominated by a pair of enormous brown eyes. Her hands glittered with the inevitable Moon rings, but she held them poised, ready for any movement, as if she were a magician trained.

Lute bowed. "Mother Portal."

The bright brown eyes locked on him with a force that nearly took him to his knees. She returned his bow with a nod of her head. "Child. Be welcome." Her voice was unexpectedly soft.

Lady Rowan thrust herself forward. "Mother Portal, this—"

But the older lady's eyes had moved, to rest upon Moonhawk.

"I had thought you were to meditate until I called you here."

"Yes, Mother," said Moonhawk, with poise.

" 'Yes, Mother'," repeated the sharp lady. "And have I called you here? Refresh my memory."

"No, Mother," Moonhawk returned, never moving her eyes from those of her interrogator.

There was a small pause before Mother Portal moved her eyes and walked across the room to the cat. "How extraordinary. No doubt you have your reasons." She extended a wire-thin hand and stroked the cat from head-top to rump. Satisfied rumbling rose in the scented air.

"So," said Mother Portal, looking down at her hand stroking the cat. "But Rowan had something of urgency to impart. What was that, Rowan?"

"Mother, this man is a Circle-breaker and an intruder. He was found within the walls of the Inner Garden." Malice glinted in Lady Rowan's dark eyes. "With Sister Moonhawk."

"Circle-breaker. That is serious," Mother Portal told the cat. She glanced up, capturing Lute's gaze. "Are you a Circle-breaker, my son?"

Lute met her eyes straightly, and held himself utterly calm. "No, Mother."

"Said plainly enough. Were you in the Inner Garden with Lady Moonhawk?"

"Yes," said Lute, and folded his lips tightly over *but*.

Mother Portal's eyes sharpened. "There were circumstances, were there? But you don't care to name yourself a fool. Pride belongs to the foolish, you know, but no matter. Lady Moonhawk."

"Mother?"

"How came this man to be in the Garden with you?"

"I was meditating upon the Garden, that its peace would fill me, when there was—discord. Only an instant—only a flicker. If I had not been one with the Garden, I would never have noticed. As it was, trance was broken. . ." She tipped her head, a trick of the pathetically young, thought Lute, watching her.

"I sought the source and touched a thought—a thought of being hunted, Mother, and a taste of desperation. So I descended into the Garden, to see if I might aid one who was being hunted upon Beltane."

"And so you found this man?"

"Yes, Mother."

"What was he doing?"

Moonhawk's lips curved upward, very slightly. "He was being invisible."

"Invisible!" That was Lady Rowan. Mother Portal spared her a glance and she subsided.

"Invisible," Moonhawk reiterated. "He did well with it, too. If I had not been looking for him, I would have passed within a yard and never known he was there."

"Unconvincing," snapped Lady Rowan, "when it most likely yourself who let him in—just as you let him in the Plaza Gate!"

"Alas," Lute said gently, "I fear you are out there, Lady. I let myself in through the gate."

"Certainly you did," she said with cordial sarcasm. "And with merely a wave of your hand."

"No," said Lute, "with a picklock." He gestured and the instrument in question appeared between his fingers—and vanished. "I've studied the old locks. The type you have on the gate is very simple. No trouble at all to pick."

"No trouble to pick." That was Lady Portal, who was moving away from the cat. She pulled a tarot deck from a fold of her robe and began to shuffle, the cards nearly as large as her small hands. She looked up, deep into Lute's eyes.

"But who showed you were to look for the Gate, I wonder?"

He moved his shoulders in an irritable shrug. "No one needs to teach me to see what is in plain sight. I had noted the gate earlier this evening. When three of your Temple were striving to herd me against the wall, I recalled its location, and made use of it."

The cards made a slight sandpapery sound in the silence.

"Lady Rowan," Mother Portal said dreamily, "you were once a novice. How many levels of spell are woven about that Gate?"

"Twenty-six, Mother."

"Twenty-six. And also the several layers of spell we have wove about the Temple entire." She shuffled in silence, her eyes on the cards, then glanced up, sharp, into Lute's face. "You interest me, child. Have you perhaps had Circle training, as I hear is sometimes offered boys in the out-country, in years when girls are few?"

He laughed; he could not stop himself.

"Respect for Mother Portal!" cried Rowan and Lute raised his hand in protest.

"Every respect for Mother Portal," he replied, bringing himself under control. He bowed to the tiny woman. "Forgive me, Mother, but Circle would not have me. My mother brought us to the Temple, she having fallen into hard times, and offered us both for service. They wanted only her daughter and turned her and me out with a loaf of bread in trade." He deliberately relaxed his shoulders, which were tense with the old bitterness.

"What came forth then?" asked Mother Portal.

He smiled at her. "Why, then, my mother sold me, Lady, to a man with clever hands who said he had need of an apprentice, and who promised to feed me and give me a trade and who paid her in good minted silver."

"He did those things?"

"Lady, he did. Only imagine my dismay to find that the trade I learned so well now makes me outlaw." He gestured and the parchment came to hand, unrolling with the weight of the ribbons and pentagram. He held it steady for her to read.

" 'By the hand of Greenlady. . .' " she said softly, and her eyes when she looked into Lute's face were knife sharp. "Lady Moonhawk, what do you make of this?"

The tall woman came a few steps forward, frowned at the proclamation. "To name an entire guild outlaw?" she said in wondering accents. "For what wrong?"

"An excellent question. Perhaps Lady Rowan may instruct us."

"Certainly," said that Lady, nervously folding her hands before her. "It was decided among Thirteen that the kitchen and hearth magicians confuse the simple, who are not trained to mark the difference between mere trickery and the true magic of those who are of the Circle. The Way is difficult enough, to the simple, and we owe them the care of removing falsehood from their path, that they not stumble because of our inattention."

"And so this—document—was drafted and posted in the city?"

"Yes, Mother."

"And it was considered too small a thing, I gather," pursued Portal, unrelentingly gentle, "with which to trouble the High Priestess of Dyan Temple?"

There was silence; a beginning of speech, cut off as Mother Portal turned back to Lute.

"Where were you bound with this thing, child?"

"To the Magician's Guildhall, Mother, to show it to the Master." He looked down at her bleakly, the hairs standing tall on his nape. If the Mother of Dyan Temple were not impervious to political maneuverings within her own Circle. . . He broke her gaze, looked up, located and pointed at Feldris.

"This man was there. He told me he was newly named Guildmaster. He said that the magicians of Dyan City are no longer within walls. I ran, thinking to lose myself in the outer rim and win free of the city tomorrow. He and three Witches pursued me across Goddess Square. I saw the gate, picked the lock. . ."

"And thus came to the Inner Garden. I see. Lady Moonhawk, take that document, if you will, and put it on my desk. Master Lute."

He started, looked down to find the tarot deck fanned face down, in a half-circle that all but hid her hand. "Draw a card."

He did so, holding it between the tips of his fingers, face still toward the floor.

"Show me," Mother Portal said, and he turned the card up, swallowing his shock, staring at the horrific black figure that leered from the creamy background.

"Do you know what card that is, Master Lute?"

He swallowed. "Death."

"Hah. And it frightens you, does it? Lady Moonhawk—what card is this?"

A quick blue glance. "The change card, Mother."

"So." She folded the deck, shot a glance at Rowan. "Bring me my pen. Master Lute, your card."

She took it from him, and the pen from Rowan, and scrawled some lines across the creamy stock before offering it back.

Lute stood still. "Mother. . ."

"Take the card, child. I've no doubt you'll find it as dangerous as you find it useful. Balance in all things is the way of the world." She thrust the card at him and perforce he took it, glancing down at the words: "The man who carries this is my emissary. Portal, Dyan Circle."

He looked at her. "I am free to go?"

"Presently," she said, frowning up at him. "You have brought me good coin, Master Lute. You must not think me ungrateful, though

I give you dubious fortune in return. Why did your master wish an apprentice?"

He lifted an eyebrow. "All masters wish an apprentice, Mother. It is one's duty, to pass on knowledge. And it is a way to keep one's own skills sharp, for there is nothing so challenging as to teach." He smiled. "So my master taught me."

"A wise man, your master. His name?"

"Cereus, who made his return to the Goddess six years ago."

"Blessed his memory. Have you an apprentice, Master Lute?"

"No one likely has come my way. Doubtless, when I have need, the Goddess will provide."

"Doubtless." She shuffled the cards again, fanned them. "Lady Moonhawk, draw a card."

The blue eyes flashed, startled. Then she extended a slender hand, pulled a card free and turned it up.

"The High Priestess." Mother Portal sighed, folded the deck and pulled from her robe a silver string with which she bound the incomplete tarot.

"Lady Rowan, there are several decks being made for me. Inform the cardmaker I will chose from those completed at full Moon. These shall stay always with me.

"Lady Moonhawk, the time has come for you to leave Circle. Master Lute, the Goddess, as you predicted, has provided you with an apprentice. I hope you will not find her hopelessly stupid, though I must tell you that she has spent all her days within these walls."

Lute stared at her, the card held loose between his fingers. "Mother, I do not understand."

"You relieve me. Suffice that you are my emissary and this is your apprentice. Return here in a year, I think, and do then as you think best."

"Mother, you cannot send one of the Inner Circle to travel the world with a—magician! It—"

"Oh," said Mother Portal, turning quick on her heel, "can I not? And what else, Lady Rowan, may I not do within the Temple where I am High Priestess?"

Lady Rowan's face had gone white. Portal nodded, sparing one last glance at Lute. "Take your apprentice and go, child. Now!"

The command voice, yet again. But this time he had no mind to resist it. He vanished the card, bent and caught up his bag, pushed past a gaping Feldris and swept his cloak from the hook by the door.

He was five strides down the hallway when he realized that Moonhawk was right beside him.

About the Authors

Maine-based writers Sharon Lee and Steve Miller teamed up in the late 80s to bring the world the story of Kinzel, a inept wizard with a love of cats, a thirst for justice, and a staff of true power. Since then, the husband-and-wife team have written dozens of short stories, and twenty-one novels, most set in their star-spanning Liaden Universe®. Before settling down to the serene and stable life of a science fiction and fantasy writer, Steve was a traveling poet, a rock-band reviewer, reporter, and editor of a string of community newspapers. Sharon, less adventurous, has been an advertising copywriter, copy editor on night-side news at a small city newspaper, reporter, photographer, and book reviewer. Both credit their newspaper experiences with teaching them the finer points of collaboration. Sharon and Steve passionately believe that reading fiction ought to be fun, and that stories are entertainment. Steve and Sharon maintain a web presence at www.korval.com

Thank you

for your interest in
and support of
our work
Sharon Lee and Steve Miller

Made in the USA
Coppell, TX
24 July 2020